MR. GRE

D0716686

by Roger Hargreaves

Mr Greedy liked to eat!

In fact Mr Greedy loved to eat, and the more he ate the fatter he became.

And the trouble was, the fatter he became the more hungry he became.

And the more hungry he became the more he ate.

And the more he ate the fatter he became.

And so it went on.

Mr Greedy lived in a house that looked rather like himself.

It was a roly-poly sort of a house.

One morning Mr Greedy awoke rather earlier than usual.

He'd been dreaming about food, as usual, and that had made him wake up feeling hungry, as usual.

So Mr Greedy got up, went downstairs and ate the most enormous breakfast.

This is what Mr Greedy had for his breakfast.

TOAST – 2 slices

CORNFLAKES – 1 packet

MILK – 1 bottle

SUGAR – 1 bowlful

TOAST – 3 slices

EGGS – 3 boiled

TOAST – 4 slices

BUTTER – 1 dish

MARMALADE – 1 pot

When he had finished his enormous breakfast, Mr Greedy sat back in his chair, smiled a very satisfied smile, and thought.

"That was a delicious breakfast," he thought to himself. "Now I wonder what would be nice to have for lunch?"

He decided in order to work up an appetite for lunch he would go for a long walk.

That morning Mr Greedy walked and walked and walked.

Then he discovered a cave.

"That's funny," he thought, "I don't remember seeing that there before."

Mr Greedy, being a curious sort of a fellow, decided to explore.

He entered the dark cave.

Inside he discovered some giant steps leading upwards.

Mr Greedy, being a curious sort of a fellow, decided to climb them.

They were very steep and very difficult to climb, but with much huffing and puffing Mr Greedy climbed up and up.

At the top of the steps Mr Greedy came to a door.

It was, without doubt, the biggest door that Mr Greedy had ever seen. And it wasn't quite shut.

Mr Greedy, being a curious sort of a fellow, decided to see what was on the other side of that door.

So Mr Greedy squeezed himself through the crack in the door, and there before him was an amazing sight.

The biggest room in the world!

The floor was as big as a field.

The table in the middle of the floor was as big as a house, and the chairs around it were as high as trees.

Mr Greedy felt very small.

Then he sniffed.

Coming from somewhere up on top of that gigantic table was the most delicious foody smell that Mr Greedy had ever smelled.

Mr Greedy sniffed again, and then decided that he must get up on to that table, so he began to climb up the leg of the enormous chair.

It was very difficult and it took him a long time, but eventually Mr Greedy stood on the table.

Everything was larger than life.

The salt and pepper pots were both as big as pillar boxes.

There was a bowl of fruit on the table, and Mr Greedy tried to lift one of the oranges.

And Mr Greedy, being Mr Greedy, took a bite out of one of the apples there.

Then he looked around.

Over on the other side of the table stood the source of that delicious smell.

A huge enormous gigantic colossal plate, and on the plate, huge enormous gigantic colossal sausages the size of pillows, and huge enormous gigantic colossal potatoes the size of beachballs, and huge enormous gigantic colossal peas the size of cabbages.

Mr Greedy hurried across the table towards the plate, and, being Mr Greedy, began to eat.

Suddenly a shadow fell across the plate, and Mr Greedy found himself being picked up by a giant hand and looking into the eyes of a real live giant.

"AND WHO," thundered the giant, "ARE YOU?"

Mr Greedy was so frightened that he could only just manage to squeak his name. "Mr Greedy," he squeaked.

The giant laughed a laugh as loud as thunder. "GREEDY BY NAME AND GREEDY BY NATURE," he bellowed. "WELL I THINK MR GREEDY THAT YOU NEED TO BE TAUGHT A LESSON!"

And what a lesson it was.

The giant made Mr Greedy eat up everything on that huge enormous gigantic colossal plate.

When he had finished, Mr Greedy felt very ill indeed, as if he would burst at any minute.

"Now," said the giant in a much quieter voice, "do you promise never to be greedy again?"

"Oh yes," moaned Mr Greedy, "I promise!"

"Very well," said the giant, "then I'll let you go."

Mr Greedy climbed down from the table and went out through the door feeling very fat and extremely miserable.

And do you know, from that day to this, Mr Greedy has kept his promise.

And do you know something else as well?

Mr Greedy doesn't look like he used to look any more.

He now looks like this, which I think suits him a lot better, don't you?

So if you know anybody who's as greedy as Mr Greedy used to be you know what to tell them, don't you?

Beware of giants!

Fantastic offers for Mr. Men fans!

Collect all your Mr. Men or Little Miss books in these superb durable collectors' cases!
Only £5.99 inc. postage and packing, these wipe-clean, hard-wearing cases will give all your Mr. Men or Little Miss books a beautiful new home!

Keep track of your collection with this giant-sized double-sided Mr. Men and Little Miss Collectors' poster.
Collect 6 tokens and we will send you a brilliant giant-sized double-sided collectors' poster! Simply tape a £1 coin to cover postage and packaging in the space provided and fill out the form overleaf.

STICK £1 COIN HERE
(for poster only)

cut along the dotted line and return this whole page

Only need a few Mr. Men or Little Miss to complete your set? You can order any of the titles on the back of the books from our Mr. Men order line on 0870 787 1724. Orders should be delivered between 5 and 7 working days.

TO BE COMPLETED BY AN ADULT

To apply for any of these great offers, ask an adult to complete the details below and send this whole page with the appropriate payment and tokens, to: MR. MEN CLASSIC OFFER, PO BOX 715, HORSHAM RH12 5WG

☐ Please send me a giant-sized double-sided collectors' poster.

AND ☐ I enclose 6 tokens and have taped a £1 coin to the other side of this page.

☐ Please send me ☐ Mr. Men Library case(s) and/or ☐ Little Miss library case(s) at £5.99 each inc P&P

☐ I enclose a cheque/postal order payable to Egmont UK Limited for £.....

OR ☐ Please debit my MasterCard / Visa / Maestro / Delta account (delete as appropriate) for £.....

Card no. ☐☐☐☐☐☐☐☐☐☐☐☐☐☐☐☐☐☐☐☐ Security code ☐☐☐

Issue no. (if available) ☐ Start Date ☐☐/☐☐/☐☐ Expiry Date ☐☐/☐☐/☐☐

Fan's name: ..... Date of birth: .....

Address: .....

.....

..... Postcode: .....

Name of parent / guardian: .....

Email for parent / guardian: .....

Signature of parent / guardian: .....

Please allow 28 days for delivery. Offer is only available while stocks last. We reserve the right to change the terms of this offer at any time and we offer a 14 day money back guarantee. This does not affect your statutory rights. Offers apply to UK only.

☐ We may occasionally wish to send you information about other Egmont children's books. If you would rather we didn't, please tick this box.

Ref: MRM 001

cut along the dotted line and return this whole page